FOXY

The Foxes of Hamilton Hills

ISBN 978-1-0980-9141-5 (paperback)
ISBN 978-1-0980-9142-2 (digital)

Christian Faith Publishing, Inc.
832 Park Avenue
Meadville, PA 16335
www.christianfaithpublishing.com

Printed in the United States of America

FOXY

The Foxes of Hamilton Hills

Joel Witmeyer

Cover Illustration by Kylea Cournoyer

Hi, I'm Cyrus. I bet you're wondering what I am. Well, I am a red fox. Have you ever seen one like me? I bet not. I live under this weird-looking building. It's quite cramped as I have five siblings who live with me. I don't like being that crowded, but I am *happy* and *blessed* with what I have.

I like to pop out of this hole and hear all the sounds. Lots of weird

noises I never heard before—chirps, loud clicks (darn photographers), and leaves crunching. I can even hear a watch ticking forty yards away.

This is my sister, Fayth. She says she is a believer. Not quite sure what she means, but she always says there is **light** at the end of the tunnel. And you know what? She's right!

Whenever I am outside, spending some time in the sun, she comes up and gives me a kiss on the nose.

Why do sisters do that? I just don't get it. I want to roll around in the mud and fight with my brothers. She keeps saying "It's because I love you, Cyrus." You know what? It makes me feel good. I'm so **grateful** for family.

9

Ah, my older brother, Samson, towers over me and has **huge** strength. We love to wrestle and play all the time. Sometimes he gets too rough and does not stop. Not sure why, since it doesn't make me feel good. But he always comes back to tell me he is **sorry**. I love Samson.

He does protect me from predators when we go hunting—only when Mom lets us pretend-hunt. We aren't old enough yet. What Mom  says goes! It's important we **obey** her. She says it's for our own good. Sometimes I don't understand, but I guess that is why they say "moms always know best."

Recently, we had to move. I was quite sad since all my friends were in the old area. Isn't it scary when you don't know anybody and you are the

new kid? I feel that way. Dad tells me to just **trust** that you have everything in you—that our **strength** comes from above. When I think about that, I feel at **peace** and everything will be all right.

My new home is great now. I have a much-bigger area to play and run. Look at this cool stick I found. Do you have a favorite toy? I would love to hear about it. Maybe we can play sometime. You can always find me on the Hamilton Hills.

Today is the big day. I'll be the new kid in school. It's a bit scary, but I know **God watches over me** and will be with me every step of

the way. My mom gave me extra hugs and kisses before I left, so that helped! Aren't moms great?

Wow, what a day! I met so many new friends. It wasn't bad after all. My favorite part was chasing my own tail ten times. Don't ask! It's a fox thing! Hope you enjoy your day! I'm going to tell Mom all about mine! I hope you do, as well.

Do you ever wish you could fly? As I'm out playing, I see the birds in the air and butterflies soaring around. My favorite is the bald eagle. They can **soar** over ten thousand feet.

Just like that eagle, I have a chance to **soar** in my own life. I can make a difference in my

family's and friends' lives, especially with my brothers and sisters. Sometimes, all that they need is a bit of **encouragement** to get through the day. What are some things you can do every day?

Sometimes, life gets hard. People are mean and say hurtful things. I do my best to **love** everyone I meet. I like to be the **light** in the darkness,

shining **love** everywhere I go. Life is what I make it, and I choose happiness!

Guess what? There is always a place where I know I am loved. You know where? It's a place called home. I love my family. We are a tribe.

Hope to See You Sometime at Hamilton Hills

About the Author

Joel Witmeyer is a photographer, a graphic artist, and more importantly, a child of God. Joel is much more of a visual person than he is a writer. He loves nature and all of God's creations.

Joel was blessed with an opportunity to follow a family of foxes. This made a perfect opprtunity for him to write a little short story and share some of his work. The idea came while he was in prayer.

For Joel, he is capturing what God has created in life. God is the true artist, and Joel is using his style to give glory to God. That is his motivation.

CPSIA information can be obtained
at www.ICGtesting.com
Printed in the USA
BVHW021320020821
613410BV00018B/669